Date Due		
MAY 1 9 1978	MAY 2 0 1968	
APR 1 7 1979		
FEB 9		
MAR 8		
SEP 1 4 1981		
MAY 0 3 1985		
DEC 1 0		
FEB 2 1987		
FEB 0 5 1988		

Udry, Janice May
  How I Faded Away

Other Books
by
Janice May Udry
•
Emily's Autumn
What Mary Jo Shared
What Mary Jo Wanted
Mary Jo's Grandmother

How I Faded Away

Janice May Udry

Pictures by
Monica De Bruyn

Albert Whitman & Company, Chicago

Library of Congress Cataloging in Publication Data
Udry, Janice May.
  How I faded away.

  (Concept books)
  SUMMARY: Unhappy and ignored at school Robbie
fades away but becomes visible when he cries or finds
something he can do well.
    [1.   School stories]   I.   De Bruyn, Monica.
II.   Title.
PZ7.U27Ho   [Fic]   75-30863
ISBN 0-8075-3416-1

How I Faded Away

Do you know what it's like
to be invisible?

I can tell you.

It's almost as bad as
people seeing you when you
don't want them to.

I know because I became
invisible at school.

When I first started to school in the first grade, I know that everybody saw me then.

The teacher and the kids noticed everything about me.

I think they noticed every single mistake I made.

"That's wrong," they said. "Can't you do it, Robbie? Aren't you finished yet?"

In the second grade, I didn't want to answer questions or ask questions anymore. I didn't like to be monitor or book-passer or anything like that anymore.

I didn't want to sing or go to the blackboard. I never wanted to play games on the playground either.

I just counted the days and minutes until school was out in the summer. I couldn't wait.

I was visible all summer.

On our vacation in the mountains
and when I visited my grandparents,
I was completely visible.

But—after school began again in September I slowly and gradually began to fade away.

The teacher could barely make me out when she took attendance first thing in the mornings.

Sometimes she frowned and said, "Robbie, I can hardly see you or hear you. Speak up! Sit up! You don't want to be counted absent, do you?"

The principal never saw me at all.
The other kids
didn't see me
anymore.

The last one to see me was
Chris Horner before he moved away.

I was only invisible at school.
As soon as I crossed the street,
ran across the yard and
in the front door at home
I was completely visible again.

My mother and father and sister
could always see me. Even if we
went out in the evening to a concert
or something, I was clearly visible.

I only began to fade on my way
to school.

I told my family that I didn't
want to go to school. But of course
they told me I had to go.

"Everyone must go to school.
It's the law," they always told me.

"Do you have to go even if you
are invisible?" I asked them.

"Being invisible is no reason
not to go to school," they said.

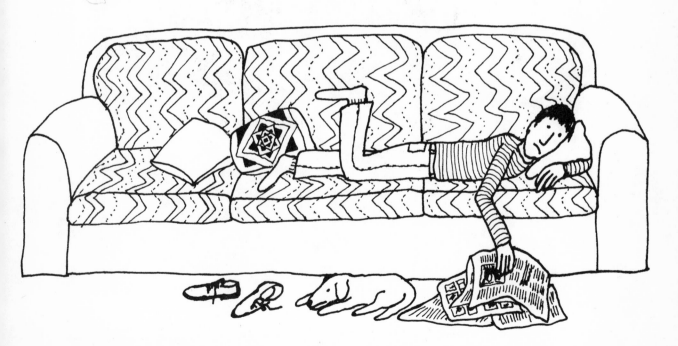

I didn't enjoy
being stepped on
or shoved.

And I didn't like people
getting in front of me
in the school cafeteria line.

"Oops. I didn't see you,"
they said.

One day
I began to cry because
I didn't like being
invisible.

And—

would you believe it?—

I slowly became visible!

With tears coming down my face,
I had to become visible.

The teacher and all the kids suddenly saw me very clearly.

"Look, Robbie is crying!" they said.

"What happened?"

"Why are you crying?"

I told them it was nothing. I said I just had a cold.

As soon as the tears stopped, I disappeared again.

Well, I'd rather be invisible than be visible crying.

Then one day, the teacher passed out recorders and music books.

Everyone got a recorder except—me.

There was one short, and since I was invisible, of course I didn't get a recorder.

This was really a disappointment because I love music. I'd been looking forward to the day when we would begin playing the recorders.

It was all I could do to keep from crying
while I listened to the others begin.

As soon as I got home,
I went to my room and began
to cry.

Then I noticed my bank
and remembered I had some
Christmas money from my aunt
left.

I wiped my eyes and opened
the bank.

I went downtown
to a music store
and bought myself
a recorder.

I started
practicing
at home.

I took the recorder to school.

And during music period
a strange thing happened.
As soon as I began to play,
I slowly became visible.

It was like the day when
I cried at school.

"Listen to Robbie," they
said.

"That's good, Robbie."

"Robbie must be a musician."

The teacher and all the kids
suddenly saw me clearly.

Sometimes I wonder if my recorder is a magic one. I guess I'll never know. But whether it's magic or not, I love to play.

I'm hardly ever invisible anymore. And even when I am, I don't care now.